Hairy Maclary's Rumpus at the Vet

Lynley Dodd

TRICYCLE PRESS
Berkeley, California

Down at the Vet's
there were all kinds of pets,
with troubles and woes
from their ears to their toes.
Sniffles and snuffles
and doses of flu,
itches and stitches
and tummy ache too.
So many animals,
watchful and wary,
and Hairy Maclary
from Donaldson's Dairy.

There were miserable dogs,
cantankerous cats,
a rabbit with pimples
and rickety rats.
Mice with the sneezes,
a goat in a rage,
and Cassie the cockatoo
locked in her cage.

Cassie had claws
and a troublesome beak.
She saw something twitch
so she gave it a
TWEAK.

She pulled it so hard
that she plucked out a hair
and Hairy Maclary
jumped high in the air.

A bowl full of mice
was bundled about.
Over it went
and the mice tumbled out.

Four fussy budgies
with Grandmother Goff
flew out of their cage
when the bottom dropped off.

Grizzly MacDuff
with a bottlebrush tail
leaped out of his basket
and over the rail.

The Poppadum kittens
from Parkinson Place
squeezed through an opening
and joined in the chase.

Barnacle Beasley
forgot he was sore.
He bumbled and clattered
all over the floor.

Then Custard the labrador,
Muffin McLay
and Noodle the poodle
decided to play.
They skidded and scampered,
they slid all around
and bottles and boxes
came tumbling down.

What a kerfuffle,
a scramble of paws,
a tangle of bodies,
a jumble of jaws.
With squawking and yowling
and mournful miaow,
they really were making
a TERRIBLE row.

Out came the Vet.
"I'll fix them," she said.
But she tripped on a lead
and fell over instead.

Geezer the goat
crashed into a cage.
He butted the bars
in a thundering rage.

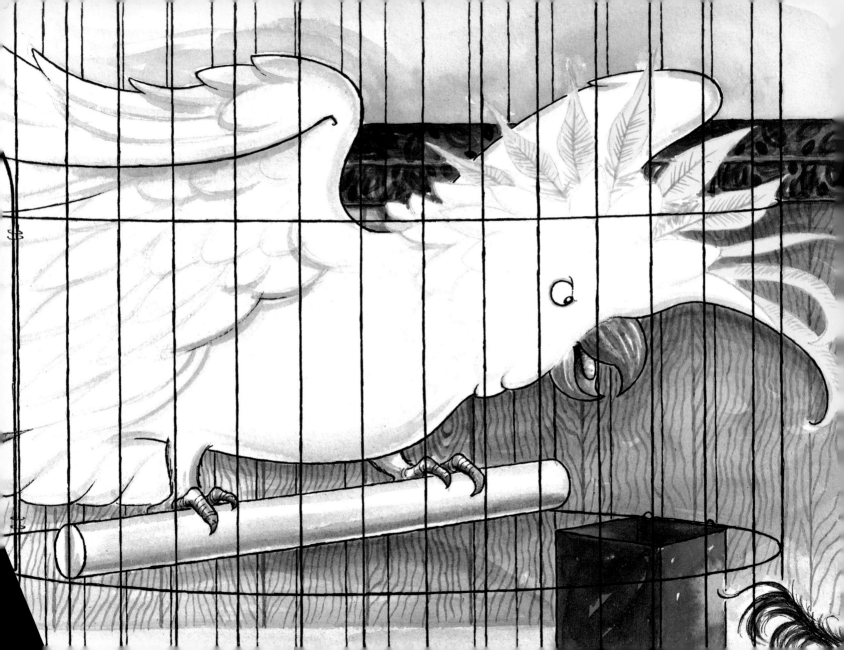

Cassie got mad.
She rattled her beak.
She saw something twitch
so she
gave
it
a…

TWEAK.

Other TRICYCLE PRESS books by Lynley Dodd
Hairy Maclary and Zachary Quack
Hairy Maclary from Donaldson's Dairy
Hairy Maclary Scattercat
Hairy Maclary's Bone
Slinky Malinki
Slinky Malinki Catflaps
Slinky Malinki, Open the Door

TRICYCLE PRESS
an imprint of Ten Speed Press
PO Box 7123
Berkeley, California 94707
www.tricyclepress.com

Library of Congress Cataloging-in-Publication Data
Dodd, Lynley.
Hairy Maclary's rumpus at the vet / Lynley Dodd.
p. cm.
Summary: A cockatoo's attack on Hairy's tail starts a chain
reaction among the animals at the vet's.
ISBN-13: 978-1-58246-094-9 / ISBN-10: 1-58246-094-9
[1. Dogs--Fiction. 2. Cockatoos--Fiction. 3. Animals--Fiction.
4. Veterinarians--Fiction. 5. Stories in rhyme.] I. Title.
PZ8.3.D637Hao 2003
[E]--dc21

2002007699

First Tricycle Press printing, 2003
Manufactured in China

3 4 5 6 7 — 13 12 11 10 09